GW00865219

MEET ALL THESE FRIENDS IN
BUZZ BOOKS:

Thomas the Tank Engine
Wind in the Willows
The Animals of Farthing Wood
Skeleton Warriors
Fireman Sam

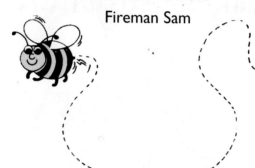

First published in Great Britain 1996 by Buzz Books
an imprint of Reed International Books
Michelin House, 81 Fulham Road, London SW3 6RB
and Auckland, Melbourne, Singapore and Toronto

Pony In My Pocket™ © 1995 Morrison Entertainment Group Inc.
Licensed by Just Licensing Limited
Illustrations by Arkadia, copyright © 1996 Reed International Books
Text copyright © 1996 Reed International Books

ISBN 1 85591 549 9

Printed in Italy by Olivotto

A Pony
Trekking Adventure

Story by Susan Allan

Illustrations by Arkadia

One rainy afternoon, all the ponies were in the stables getting ready to go out to play in the paddock.

"What shall we do today, then?" asked Cavalier gloomily as he watched the drip-drip of rain from the roof.

"I don't know," replied Misty, scuffing her hoofs.

"Who wants to race me to the barn and back?" offered Bonnie.

Not one pony replied.

"We could go to the farm and see if they need any help," suggested Dolly. All the ponies looked forlornly at the clouds.

Suddenly Toby trotted in from the yard. He stopped in his tracks.

"What's the matter with all of you?" he demanded when he saw their miserable faces.

The ponies looked at each other and started to explain.

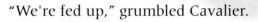

"We're fed up," grumbled Cavalier.

Bonnie continued: "We can't play out in the paddock because of the rain and there's nothing else for us to do."

"But there's lots for us to do," said Toby. He led his friends out of the stables.

"Look, it's stopped raining now."

He turned to the ponies. They still looked a little gloomy.

"I think I know what we need!" he said excitedly.

All the ponies listened eagerly.

"We need to go on a day trip and have some fun!"

"Yes!" cheered the ponies, as they began to talk to each other about what they would like to do.

"I've always wanted to visit the seaside," said Cavalier to Dolly.

"A trip to the city!"

"What about the mountains?"

Toby stood quietly and wondered what would be the best idea. Everyone seemed to want to do different things. They would never find something that every pony would enjoy.

"Pony Trekking," said Misty quietly.

Toby turned to her. "Did you say Pony Trekking?"

Misty nodded her head. "I went once when I was a young filly, and it was great fun. Everyone will enjoy it."

"What a wonderful idea! Listen everyone," Toby called. "Misty has come up with the perfect trip. Let's go on a Pocketville Pony Trek. We'll go tomorrow if the weather is fine."

All the ponies cheered in agreement.

That evening at the stables, as the light began to fail, and the ponies tucked themselves up warmly for the night, the talk was all about their trip.

Bonnie was so excited she thought she would never sleep.

"Get into bed and I'll tell you all about Pony Trekking," said Misty kindly. "It's great fun," she explained. "We'll take a packed lunch, and set off early in the morning. We'll trek across fields, over hills, along rivers … but the best part is that we're going to visit Apple Wood."

"What's Apple Wood?" asked Bonnie.

"It's a beautiful forest filled with every sort of tree and plant you can imagine. It's a very special place. In fact some ponies say that it is a magic forest where tiny wild ponies live. Though no-one has ever seen them, legend has it that they are guardians of the forest and all its inhabitants."

"What a lovely tale …" murmured
Bonnie as her eyes closed and she drifted
off to sleep.

The next day the ponies awoke to brilliant sunshine.

After a hasty breakfast they all gathered together outside in the yard.

"We're off on our first Trek everyone," called Misty. "You must always keep sight of the pony in front of you, so you don't lose your way. Follow me." Off the friends set on their Pony Trek.

The ponies made their way across
farmland towards the hills in the distance.
Flat tracks gave way to bridleways and
fields gave way to beautiful rolling hills.

The sun shone warmly on the ponies'
backs and birds raced across the sky. They
trotted on towards a wood nestled at the
bottom of a valley.

"This is wonderful," sighed Cavalier happily. "This was such a good idea." He smiled at Toby.

Apple Wood

"Keep up," called Misty to the stragglers at the back of the group.

"We're going to trek through Apple Wood now," she said. "Look out for all the lovely wild flowers you'll see there."

Deep in the wood, Bonnie couldn't
believe her eyes. She had never seen such
a beautiful forest. Apple trees mingled
with oak and birch trees. At ground level,
bluebells and other wild flowers covered
the earth in a colourful carpet.

Friendly bees swarmed collecting pollen, and a little squirrel darted up a nearby tree. Bonnie stopped to watch as he scuttled towards his mate across a branch, when she felt something light on her nose. She looked down to see that a brightly coloured butterfly had landed delicately on her muzzle.

Within a moment it had fluttered off – Bonnie followed it.

She trotted past a family of rabbits, as the butterfly led her on.

"Where are you taking me?" she wondered, as it flitted ahead of her.

She continued along a narrow track
until she found her way into an opening
in the trees, where a small pond was
bathed in yellow sunlight. She stopped
for a moment to drink when she realised
that she had forgotten Misty's advice. She
was completely alone and had long since
lost her fellow Trekkers.

"Oh, dear," she thought to herself, "I've
been gone for ages. My friends must be
missing me by now." But Bonnie wasn't
scared. The wood felt so friendly that she
could not be worried.

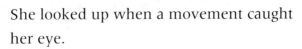

She looked up when a movement caught her eye.

"Goodness," she said to herself. "That looked like a pony – I'm sure I saw the swish of a tail, and a hind hoof. Perhaps I'm not as far from the other ponies as I thought I was." Bonnie made her way to follow her friends.

On she went, through a little stream, then past a huge fir-tree, when she stopped and looked around. The pony she was following had disappeared. She glanced down to see small hoof prints in the damp earth leading ahead of her up a bank. "What a tiny pony," she thought to herself. "It must be Toby or Dolly. I'd better hurry to catch them up."

Bonnie trotted up the hill, when she glimpsed a white pony in the distance.

"Cavalier!" she called. "It's Bonnie." But the pony didn't stop.

As Bonnie rounded the corner she suddenly saw the bright spring sunlight filtering through the trees at the edge of the wood.

"This must be the way out," she said
to herself and cantered out into the wide
open fields.

There, a little way ahead of her, were
her Pony Trekking friends, making their
way towards home.

Bonnie raced to catch up with them.

"Hello!" she called. "I'm sorry I
disappeared, but I was enjoying Apple
Wood so much that I forgot the time and
lost you all. Luckily I caught sight of
Cavalier in the distance and followed him
out of the wood. I'm sorry I'm so late,"

All the other ponies turned to her.

"Bonnie, what are you talking about?" asked Toby, confused. "We'd only just got to Apple Wood when Cavalier got a stone in his shoe, so he's gone back to the stables ahead of us. He never went into Apple Wood."

"And what do you mean by late?" enquired Misty. "That was only a few moments ago – we didn't even realise you were missing."

Bonnie looked puzzled. She was quite sure that she had spent more than five minutes in Apple Wood. Then a thought came to her as she remembered the legend Misty had told her about. If it wasn't one of her friends she was following, she thought she might know which pony it had been … one of the guardian ponies of Apple Wood!